Taking
The Land

Joshua and the Victory at Jericho

'Bringing God's Word to *LIFE*!'

Retold by Julie A. Voudrie
Illustrated by Bryant Owens

Other Bible Storybook Companions currently available:

Mighty Man vs. Almighty God: The Story of David & Goliath

The Prayer of a Righteous Man: The Story of Daniel & The Lion's Den

Spying Out The Land: Joshua's Spies in Jericho

Taking The Land: Joshua and the Victory at Jericho
Retold by: Julie A. Voudrie
Illustrations: Bryant Owens
Sidebars: Dr. Lee Magness
Managing Editor: Jeffrey D. Voudrie
Published by Shepherd's Press™
a part of Shepherd's Tales™
Copyright © 1995 Shepherd's Tales™

ISBN 1-886858-23-3
UPC 789297005041

Printed in USA

For information:
Shepherd's Tales
P.O. Box 1911
Johnson City, TN 37605-1911
1-800-621-8904

From the owners of Shepherd's Tales™ *:*

Welcome to the Shepherd's Tales™ family! We hope this book brings you many hours of enjoyment. Shepherd's Tales™ is a family-owned company with a desire to bring God's Word to life in a way that ignites the imagination, while more importantly, illuminating the spirit.

Although these books are designed as companions to Shepherd's Tales™ Bible Story Cassettes, we couldn't possibly include thirty minutes of dialogue into 32 pages! For younger children, these books will fuel their imagination as they listen to the story on tape. For older children, the additional information found in the side-bars will give them a more in-depth look into spiritual truths as well as the history of biblical times. Scripture references included in the side-bars will also encourage further Bible study.

When combined with reading the biblical text, the exciting listening experience of Shepherd's Tales™ Bible Story Cassettes and the vivid illustrations of Shepherd's Tales™ Bible Storybook Companions will create a deeper understanding of who God is and how He works in the lives of His people. We hope you enjoy your journey into the incredible lives of God's people and pray that His word will be brought to life in the heart of your family.

Jeff and Julie Voudrie

It was early morning as the Israelite officers gathered in Joshua's tent. After forty years of wandering in the wilderness, the Israelites were camped just a few miles from the Jordan River and the border of Canaan, their Promised Land. Now that Moses was dead and Joshua had taken his place, the officers were anxious to hear their new leader's plans.

"This is a very exciting time for me," said Joshua after greeting his men. "I've called you together this morning to give you instructions for crossing the Jordan!"

The men shouted for joy. They were finally entering the Promised Land! After Joshua told them how to prepare the people for the crossing, the officers were concerned, knowing the Jordan was at flood stage and would be very difficult to cross. Nor could they ignore the mighty city of Jericho that awaited them just a few miles on the other side of the river.

"God will make a way for us to cross the Jordan," said Joshua reassuringly. "And as for Jericho, I've secretly sent two of our best soldiers, Micah and Benjamin, into Jericho as spies. God will show us his plan for taking Jericho when we need to know it and not before."

The officers left Joshua's tent to carry out their orders.

Soon the entire Israelite camp was buzzing with the news. A man named Eliam and his family heard the news from Caleb, the oldest leader in their tribe of Judah. Caleb was well-respected because many years before, he and Joshua had been spies together.

"I don't know how we'll cross the Jordan River," said Caleb. "But our Lord made a way for us to cross the Red Sea, so I'm sure He'll make a way for us to cross the Jordan."

After Caleb left, Eliam's family talked about what crossing the Jordan would mean to them.

"Does this mean we won't have to live in tents anymore?" asked Eliam's daughter, Hannah.

"Don't get your hopes up too soon," chuckled her father. "Just because we enter Canaan doesn't mean we'll get to settle down right away. First, we most possess the land God has given us."

"What do you mean, 'possess the land'?" asked his son, Shimone.

"Well, other people are living in Canaan right now — wicked, evil people who serve other gods and hate the Almighty God," answered Eliam. "Canaan belongs to God and He wants to take it back, cleansing it from the sins of the Canaanites. He's promised us the land as our inheritance, as long as we continue to obey Him."

"And obey Him we shall," added Shimone's mother, Abigail.

With great anticipation they joined the rest of Israel in packing their tents. About two million people made up the twelve tribes of Israel, so there was a great bustle of activity as the people prepared to move the camp.

Even though the Israelites were eager to enter the Promised Land, they were afraid of facing the Canaanites. Would God deliver those savage people into their hand? And what about crossing the flooded river? These were some of the Israelites' worries as the time came to cross the Jordan.

Joshua gave orders for the priests carrying the Ark of the Lord to lead the people across the Jordan. The whole camp of the Israelites held their breath as the priests stepped up to the river's edge.

Would Joshua's words come to pass? Could he hear from God as Moses had? Perhaps these were some of the questions in the people's minds before the priests took their first step into the raging river.

Splash went the water as the priest stepped into the Jordan. And suddenly, the waters flowing downstream were cut off and stood in a great heap some distance away! The Israelites could hardly believe it. God had dried up the Jordan for them to cross, so they wouldn't even have to get their feet wet!

They no longer doubted Joshua's ability to be their leader. And they knew without a doubt that God was going before them to defeat their enemies in Canaan.

What do these stones mean?

Just before the Jordan began to flow again, a representative from each tribe shouldered a large stone from the riverbed and piled them near their first encampment in Canaan.

What do these stones mean? That's what God hoped future Israelites would ask as they passed that mound of weathered stones. Then parents would remember to tell their children how God had led them into the Promised Land.

God had given many memorials. The Passover meal reminded them of their deliverance from bondage, a pot of manna of God's sustenance in the wilderness, a rod of God's authority, two stone tablets of God's law, and a bronze snake of God's forgiveness.

Christians also have reminders of God's care. One is the Lord's Supper, a memorial of Jesus' death on the cross. It reminds us how God rescued us from the kingdom of darkness and led us into the Promised Land of eternal life. –Dr. Lee Magness (See Joshua 4, Hebrews 9:3,4 Numbers 21:4-9 & 1 Corinthians 11:23-26)

The miraculous crossing of the Jordan only increased the doubts of the people of Jericho. They knew Almighty God had dried up the Red Sea for the Israelites long ago, but that had always seemed so far away. How could they ignore the unleashing of God's power in their river, the Jordan? Surely nothing was impossible for the Israelites and their God.

Rahab, the woman who had hid the spies, was in the marketplace with her mother when the news of the Israelites crossing the Jordan reached Jericho.

"I hope you did the right thing by protecting those Israelite spies a few days ago," said her mother anxiously. "What if our neighbors find out you hid them to save our family?"

"They won't find out, Mama, if we don't panic!" whispered Rahab.

As they hurried home, Rahab also wondered if she had done the right thing in hiding the spies. But now was not the time for second-guessing. Rahab would not only have to keep herself calm, but her mother as well. The last thing she needed was the suspicion of her neighbors.

After being in the Promised Land for a few days, Eliam and his family went to Caleb's tent to celebrate the Passover meal. After they ate, everyone gathered around the crackling fire as Caleb began to speak. He talked about the very first Passover in Egypt and how God had set them free from their slavery. Caleb could hardly put his joy into words, now that Israel was finally in the Promised Land.

"Caleb," asked Shimone shyly, "why is being in the Promised Land so important? We still have to live in tents and eat manna. What's really changed?"

Caleb smiled thoughtfully as he began to explain how long ago, God promised to give the land of Canaan to Abraham's children, the Israelites. But first, they had to become slaves in another country. One day the sins of the people in Canaan would be more than God could bare. He would bring back Abraham's children to drive out the wicked Canaanites and give them the land as their own.

Caleb went on to explain how Israel became a mighty nation in Egypt, but how they also became slaves. After hundreds of years in slavery, God raised up a man named Moses to deliver the Israelites from their bondage. Only after suffering through horrible plagues did the Egyptians finally let the Israelites go.

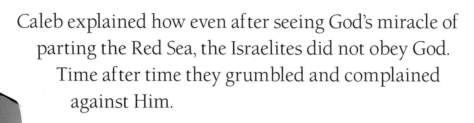

Caleb explained how even after seeing God's miracle of parting the Red Sea, the Israelites did not obey God. Time after time they grumbled and complained against Him.

Caleb described the time he and Joshua, along with ten other men, were sent as spies into Canaan. They saw mighty giants and walled cities. But in spite of the large number of crops, green fields and flowing streams they found, the other ten spies did not think that God could give them the land.

"The other spies could only see the giants," said Caleb. "They forgot God's promise to give us this land. When we returned, the other spies said, 'We can't take the land.'

"So our people rebelled against God and said, 'Let's go back to Egypt where we'll be safe.' Joshua and I just couldn't believe it. We told them, 'This is a very good land. Don't be afraid and turn back. God is with us and will give us the land.' "

"So what did the people do?" asked a child.

"They wouldn't listen to us. God was very angry and said, 'You will wander in the desert until all who have sinned against me this day are dead. Then your children will possess the land.' "

"That must have been a very sad day for Israel," said Shimone.

"It was the saddest day of my life," sighed Caleb. "Now children, you must remember we are not here today because we deserve to be. Because the Canaanites are very evil and they hate Almighty God, He has chosen us to take back the land and claim it as our own."

"Now that we're in the Promised Land, how will God drive out the Canaanites?" asked Shimone.

"I'd imagine that God will start with Jericho," replied Caleb.

"As to how He'll do it, we can only wait and see."

Camped between the Jordan and Jericho, Israel observed three important ceremonies. They built a monument of twelve stones, a reminder of how God had led them into Canaan. Second, they celebrated the Passover, looking back forty years to the Exodus when God led them out of Egypt.

The third ceremony reminded the Israelites of the covenant promise God made with Abraham. The ceremony was circumcision, the sign of the covenant with Abraham, a minor surgery (when performed on eight-day-old boys).

The Israelites had not performed circumcision in the wilderness, partly for religious, partly for hygienic reasons. Now within sight of a formidable military threat, the army of Israel was temporarily incapacitated. Circumcision was a sign of their faith in God just as it had been for Abraham centuries before. –Dr. Lee Magness (see Genesis 17:19-14,Deut. 30:6,Joshua 5:2-14 & Romans 2:28,29)

Back in Jericho, Rahab and her mother were getting more nervous and anxious with every passing day.

"Do you think they'll keep their promise Rahab?" her mother asked, looking at the scarlet cord still hanging from their window. "They may have forgotten all about you!"

"I don't think so. They pledged their lives to save our family if I kept their visit here a secret. Surely they won't forget," said Rahab hopefully. "When the Israelites do attack, I'll go get our family together. We won't be able to let anyone else in the house with us."

"Just be careful Rahab," cried her mother. "I'd hate for the our own people to kill us before the Israelites get a chance."

Not long after the Israelites celebrated the Passover, Joshua decided to walk out of the camp and take a closer look at Jericho.

On his way, he ran into his old friend Caleb. After greeting each other, they talked about how God had promised Joshua He would always be with him and make the Israelites victorious over the people of Canaan.

"Do you think much has changed here since our last visit?" asked Caleb.

"This time the Canaanites are afraid of us!" answered Joshua. He told Caleb about the two spies he had sent into Jericho and what they had seen. After the two friends said good-bye, Joshua continued on to scout out Jericho.

All was quiet now that Joshua had left behind the hustle and bustle of the camp. Not far away in the distance he could see the mighty city of Jericho. He knew that only God could deliver Jericho into their hands, but what was His plan?

"Lord, how do you want us to take such a well-fortified city?" prayed Joshua quietly.

Suddenly, he saw the most amazing sight! A man, but no ordinary man, stood before Joshua. The man was dressed in dazzling white. His face had the radiance of the sun and in his hand was a drawn sword. Joshua carefully walked up to where the man was standing.

"Are you for us or for our enemies?" asked Joshua nervously.

"I am for neither; I am on the side of the Lord," replied the man. "I've come as commander of the armies of the Living God."

As Joshua fell to the ground in worship, the commander of the Lord's army gave Joshua God's plan for taking the city of Jericho. When Joshua returned to the camp, he immediately began putting God's plan into action.

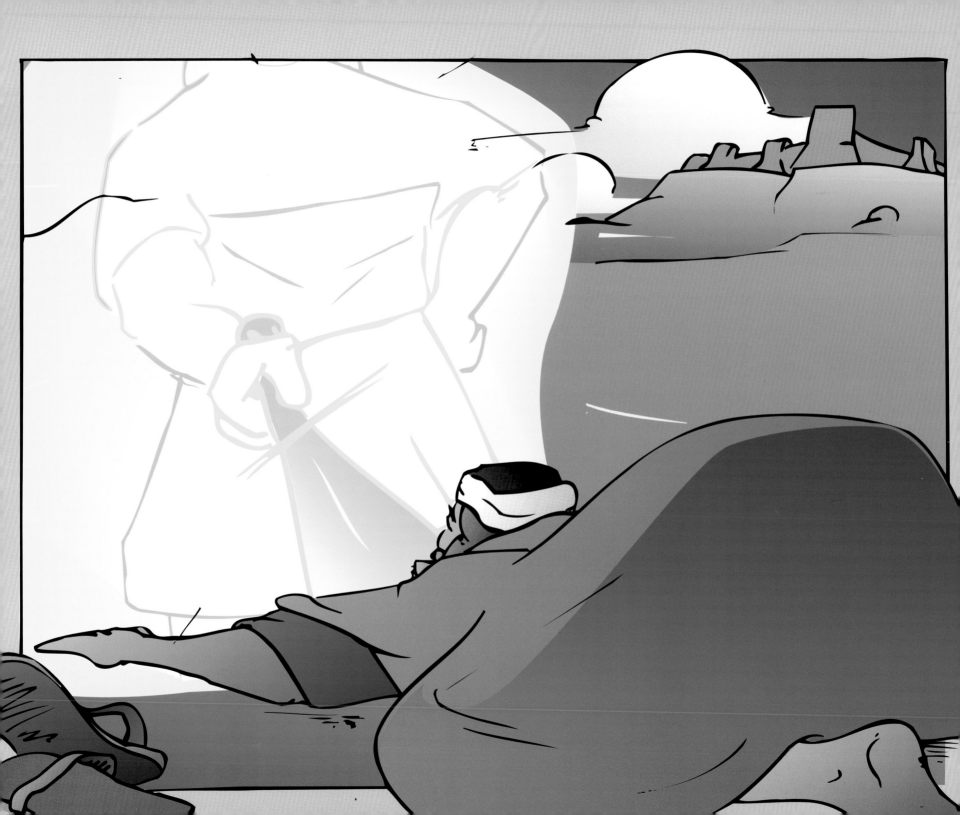

The next day, the people of Jericho awoke to a very scary sight. From the top of the city wall they could see the army of Israel marching toward their city. As the people began to panic, an eerie sound filled the air. Rahab wondered what the strange sound could be as she returned home after telling her family to come to her house.

"What are the Israelites doing?" asked Rahab as she closed the door behind her and joined her mother at the window. They saw an armed guard marching in front of seven priests blowing trumpets made of ram's horns. This was the eerie sound Rahab had heard.

"More priests are marching behind them carrying something on poles that looks like a box covered with a blue cloth," said her mother, somewhat confused.

"Mama!" said Rahab excitedly, "it's the Ark of the Covenant, where the presence of their God dwells. It's made of pure gold and anyone who touches it dies instantly!"

"Their God must be a very holy God!" said her mother in amazement "And look — after the ark there's the rest of the soldiers, not saying a single word. They're all so quiet—"

"–except for the priests blowing their trumpets," added Rahab. "I just hope we'll be safe!"

Once a day for six days the army of Israel marched around Jericho. On the seventh day, the army got up early in the morning and gathered together before setting out for Jericho. After giving them their final instructions, Joshua shared some parting words of encouragement.

"Before we entered this land," said Joshua solemnly, "God said, 'Every place where you walk, every place where you step, I have given it to you. No one will be able to stand up against you. I will never leave you nor forsake you.' Men, be strong and courageous. Do not be afraid, for the Lord your God will be with you wherever you go!"

Filled with faith, the men let out a great shout.

"It's time to go, men," shouted Joshua. "Remember, the battle belongs to the Lord!"

"The battle belongs to the Lord!" the army shouted back.

"Now —- off to Jericho!" exclaimed Joshua excitedly.

And off to Jericho they marched.

When the people of Jericho saw the army marching around the city earlier than usual, they became even more afraid than they had been before. This was the seventh day they had watched the silent soldiers encircle their walled city and they couldn't take much more.

Jericho had been attacked before, but never like this. They knew they weren't just facing the Israelites; they were facing Almighty God himself.

Worshipping their many gods gave them no peace when they needed it the most. For centuries the people of Jericho had been a wicked and evil people, committing every imaginable sin and horrible act in pursuit of their idolatry.

God's righteous judgement was about to consume them and they could feel it. With all her family gathered in her house, Rahab and her mother watched the Israelites from the relative safety of her window.

When the army was almost through marching the seventh time, Rahab noticed some of the soldiers looking up at her window.

"The rest of the family is getting nervous," cried Rahab's mother. "Something big is about to happen. I can just feel it!"

"I know what you mean, Mama. I can feel it too. But no matter what happens, we've got to stay inside this house, like the spies told us to."

Right then, they noticed something strange had happened outside. "The army has stopped marching," exclaimed Rahab. "It's like they're waiting—"

"Waiting for what?" cried her mother.

When the Israelites crossed into Canaan, they entered a land dominated by well-fortified cities, well-armed warriors and a despicable religion — Baalism. Although Canaanites worshiped many gods and goddesses, their chief god was Baal, the sender of rain, the giver of fertile crops, numerous flocks and large families.

Baalism included prostitution, "worshippers" committing sexual immorality with priestesses. Another act of worship was child sacrifice. Just as they brought the firstfruits of their crops and herds, so the Canaanites brought their firstborn children as physical sacrifices to Baal. A third characteristic of Baalism was snake worship, which some connect with Satanism.

Even after Jericho fell and the Canaanites were defeated, Baalism lived on, tempting Israelites away from the worship of God. In a sense Baalism is not dead. The temptation to worship other gods (including possessions and power) and to sexual immorality are with us even today. In the power of God we must continue to "take the land", to maintain faith in God and obedience to God's will alone. –Dr. Lee Magness (See Judges 2:10-15, Jeremiah 32:32-35 & Romans 6:11-14)

Suddenly the sound of the seven trumpets of the seven priests split the air in a long, ear-piercing blast. Then Joshua shouted his final command to the Israelite army:

"Shout! For the Lord has given you the city!"

And after being silent for so many days, the Israelite army shouted with all their might and let forth a great and awesome shout. The people in Jericho froze in absolute terror at the overpowering sound. But soon there was another sound that grabbed their attention, and a sudden sensation that something was terribly wrong.

A low rumble began and the ground started shaking under their feet. Suddenly, something like a violent earthquake shook the town of Jericho. The walls they had put their faith in began to crumble. In a matter of seconds the once massive walls fell tumbling to the ground with a mighty crash.

"The walls of the city are destroyed! Let's take this city for God!" shouted the commanders. And immediately the army of Israel rushed the helpless city.

Joshua called for the two spies, Micah and Benjamin, and told them to bring out Rahab and her family, just as they had promised. They ran over the rubble of stones and rock, wondering how Rahab could have survived the destruction of the city walls. But as Micah looked up, he had the answer.

"I can't believe it!" exclaimed Micah. "There's only one section of the walls still standing and the scarlet cord is hanging in the window!"

As they ran up to Rahab's window, Micah and Benjamin shouted to see if Rahab and her family were safe.

"We're fine!" smiled Rahab, leaning out of her window. "God has kept our lives from death, just as you promised!"

"Praise God!" exclaimed the two spies. They led Rahab and her family to safety while the rest of the army carried out God's judgement on the wicked city.

That night, after the victory at Jericho, all the people of Israel rejoiced and praised God for the great things He had done. Eliam's family was standing together with Caleb when Joshua walked up to greet them. He explained that because of Rahab's bravery in hiding their spies, she and her family had been given a safe place to live, right outside the camp.

"I'd imagine that Rahab has learned a great lesson in faith today," smiled Caleb.

"And may today be a lesson to us all," added Joshua. "When we're on the Lord's side, mighty walls can be brought down and the enemy destroyed if we depend on God and put our whole trust in Him."

The fame of God's victory that day has lived through the ages and gives us hope that as we are obedient to Him, God will be victorious in our own lives. And that as we fight His battles, He goes before us to defeat the enemy.

Shepherd's Tales™ Bible Storybook Companions:

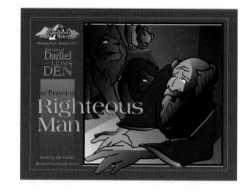

Shepherd's Tales™ Bible Story Cassettes:

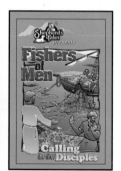